Christopher Columbus

FROM VISION TO VOYAGE

Christopher Columbus

FROM VISION TO VOYAGE

by JOAN ANDERSON

photographs by GEORGE ANCONA

Dial Books for Young Readers New York

To Josep Maria Folch, with deep gratitude—J.A.
To Manel Barcelo, a perfect Columbus—G.A.

*This book would not have been possible without the generous
support and cooperation of Iberia Airlines of Spain.
Others who helped this project become a reality are:
Gisela Krent, Casting Director · Janine Ronsmans, Spain 92 ·
Josep Maria Folch, Gran Teatro del Liceo, Barcelona ·
Irene Peypoch, Maritime Museum, Barcelona · Betina Pons, Barcelona
Tourist Agency · Rafael Conde, Archives of Aragon · Dolores Florensa,
Library of Municipal History, Barcelona · Pilar Vico, Tourist Office of Spain ·
Teresa Sil, Costumer · Manuel Gutierrez, Del Quinto Centenario ·
Doreen Metzner, Spain 92 · Valle Ordonez Carbajal, Spain 92*

Published by Dial Books for Young Readers · A Division of Penguin Books USA Inc.
375 Hudson Street · New York, New York 10014

Text copyright © 1991 by Joan Anderson
Photographs copyright © 1991 by George Ancona
All rights reserved · Design by Amelia Lau Carling
Printed in the U.S.A.
First Edition
1 3 5 7 9 10 8 6 4 2

Library of Congress Cataloging in Publication Data
Anderson, Joan.
Christopher Columbus: from vision to voyage/
by Joan Anderson; photographs by George Ancona.
p.   cm.
Summary: Traces the life of Columbus from his being
a merchant in Genoa through his accomplishments as a
navigator, mapmaker, and explorer.
ISBN 0-8037-1041-0 (trade). —ISBN 0-8037-1042-9 (library)
1. Columbus, Christopher—Juvenile literature.
2. Explorers—America—Biography—Juvenile literature.
3. Explorers—Spain—Biography—Juvenile literature.
[1. Columbus, Christopher. 2. Explorers.]
I. Ancona, George, ill. II. Title.
E111.A5 1991   970.01′5—dc20   [B]   [920]   90-27305   CIP   AC

Translated excerpts from Columbus's journals appearing on pages 24–25
and 45 are taken from *Admiral of the Ocean Sea: A Life of Christopher Columbus,*
by Samuel Eliot Morison, copyright 1942, © 1970 by Samuel Eliot Morison,
by permission of Little, Brown and Company, pages 24, 25, 41, 97, and 154.

Author's Note

This book is about a man of great valor—one who single-handedly changed the course of world history.

So many historical figures seem larger than life. The myths that have grown up around them are so grand that people tend to see them as almost superhuman. After studying the life of Columbus, it became clear to me that he was in many ways an ordinary man, but one who had the sea in his veins and dreams in his head. His attributes included a vivid imagination, great curiosity, tremendous energy, the courage to stand by his beliefs, and the willingness to take risks. None of these characteristics alone is very unusual. But put them all together, add some twists of fate and a little luck, and you have the ingredients for greatness.

nward!" the captain shouted from the stern of the *Santa Maria* as the ship's crew loosened the lines that held her snugly to the wharf.

There were but few bystanders on the dock that early-August morning in 1492 when the three small caravels slid quietly from their moorings. The captain, Christopher Columbus, gripped the rail tightly as he gazed back at the little town of Palos, in the southwest corner of Spain. Columbus had spent a lifetime working toward this day. Now that it had finally arrived, he was anxious to hoist the sails and start his voyage.

Up until that time, no other navigator had dared to venture far on the mysterious Ocean Sea, the great body of water west of Europe and Africa. But Columbus was no typical sailor. Bored with sailing around the Mediterranean that he knew so well, he longed to explore oceans still uncharted and unknown.

"Onward!" he shouted again, this time to rally his crew that, unlike Columbus, was very uncertain about the outcome of the voyage. "We shall now see where the spices grow!" Already he imagined himself in the far-off Indies, a place no one thought could be reached by sea. No one, that is, before Christopher Columbus.

Gazing at the fast-disappearing shoreline, Columbus remembered the struggle that had brought him to this moment.

1459

A grin spread across the captain's face. He was reminded of his birthplace—Genoa, Italy—and the dingy, stuffy confines of his family's weaving shop. The small workroom, hidden in an alleyway far from the central part of town, was a dismal place for an eight-year-old boy who longed to be down by the bustling waterfront. There he could see the Arab captains unloading silks and spices, shipwrights repairing hulls, and hear sailors speaking in foreign tongues or singing sea chanteys as they worked.

Instead, Christopher was forced to sit day in and day out, surrounded by piles of freshly sheared wool to be cleaned and bunched by himself and his three brothers. He found relief from this monotonous work by gazing out the window at the harbor off in the distance. But then his mother would scold him.

"Christoforo," she would say with exasperation, "why is it that you are always staring out the window instead of tending to your work? Your basket of wool sits piled high, while your brothers' baskets are nearly empty. Always you are lost in your dreams!"

The eight-year-old boy was puzzled when his mother chided him. After all, he had been baptized in the name of Saint Christopher, who carried travelers safely across mighty waters. It seemed clear to him that the one place he truly belonged was on the wharf, among men of the sea.

"Someday," Christopher told himself with great determination, "I will sail aboard one of those ships!"

1463

Then, several years later, just when it seemed unbearable to spend one more day stuck in a weaver's shop, Christopher's father took him aside.

"Christoforo," his father said sternly, "since you spend more time on the docks than working here, I've decided to send you away." The elder Columbus paused just long enough for his son's heart to skip a beat. "You will become my agent," his father continued, "and sell the cloth we make here."

Christopher could hardly contain his joy, but he stifled his feelings, worried that his father might take back this magnificent offer.

"Hire yourself aboard one of those ships that you love so much, take the cloth that we weave, and sell it to the merchants in the ports your ship calls at," he said. "I expect you to come back with a tidy sum so that we may be rewarded for our efforts."

Christopher wasted no time finding a vessel whose captain was happy to employ an eager, strong lad. His years of watching sailors and questioning captains would help him as he set sail for the first time. The sturdy wooden merchant ships needed all available hands to get them under way. Christopher willingly pitched in, lining up with the brawny crew to hoist the heavy sails. Eventually the sounds of flapping canvas filled the air and water rushed along the sides of the sea-bound vessel. Christopher climbed the rigging and watched all the activity below.

Nothing can be more exciting than setting out on a voyage, he thought, and forever after, nothing was. The young mariner with a yearning to expand his horizons only looked back once—to see the tiny world he was leaving behind.

1463-70

He traveled to far-flung ports that captivated his imagination—Marseilles, Chios, Tunis, Barcelona, Carthage, and Lisbon—all exotic locations to a young dreamer who could now add solid facts to his fantasies.

Just as the pitch and roll of the ship created drama each day at sea, so the hustle and bustle of weltering seaports filled him with wonder, and, as he sold his family's cloth, filled his pocketbook with money. He needed to remind himself that his primary task was to be a salesman, and he quickly learned how to do that—not with words, because he couldn't speak the languages in these foreign ports, but with hand-talk, wit, and a great deal of charm.

However, the real excitement was aboard ship, where he could satisfy his appetite for all things nautical. He would try his hand at any chore, from swabbing decks to tending the galley fire, to tying knots and hauling anchor. Anxious to please and impress his superiors, he listened hard and reacted quickly. Sudden squalls demanded deft timing in the handling of sails. Split-second action was needed to batten down hatches or change the ship's course in a storm. He would rather stand a double watch than sleep. From his perch in the crow's nest high above the decks, he could warn the crew of dangerous sandbars and record in his mind the jagged coastline that would eventually be inscribed on his hand-made maps.

From the very first, Christopher felt privileged to witness what others could not. It was one thing to be on shore, looking out to sea, and quite another matter to be at sea, looking landward. He brought home money and presents from these early trips, and images of undiscovered locales that whetted his enthusiasm for further exploration.

Christopher never stayed home for long. As the years went on, there was little left for him to return to in Genoa. His father had moved the family business to Savona because Genoa was becoming a less important port for merchants and navigators. Now a man in his early twenties, Christopher was no longer an apprentice sailor, but a seasoned navigator with a good reputation among sea captains. They were more than eager to enlist him for their longer, more treacherous voyages. His ability to use the latest instruments, like the quadrant and the astrolabe, coupled with the compass he seemed to carry in his head, made him a valuable part of any crew. Christopher could find the right route in the middle of the sea as if there were a clearly marked path. Similarly, a quick glance at the night sky would tell him what kind of weather to expect. When Columbus was aboard, there was little fear of getting lost in dense fog or murky seas. His memory and senses were so keen that he could recall the shape of any harbor or cove, once seen.

Each voyage was a chance for Columbus to fine-tune his seamanship. Each new sight, or trade wind, or school of fish, or passing vessel only increased his love of the sea. While most sailors were content simply to arrive safely in a port of call, Columbus saw every voyage as an opportunity to uncover the secrets of the world.

He had long since left the contained, crowded Mediterranean, which held little mystery, and signed on for longer and longer voyages beyond the Straits of Hercules. Unlike other navigators, Columbus was not afraid to venture away from the coastal waters of Europe and Africa.

1476

It was during one of these trips, on a ship carrying a valuable cargo, that his vessel was attacked by an enemy fleet. Columbus, although wounded by a bullet, dove clear of the sinking ship, grabbed onto a piece of wreckage, and, mustering every bit of strength, swam six miles to the shores of Portugal.

Exhausted and disoriented, he picked himself up from the sandy beach and gradually made his way to nearby Lisbon, where his brother Bartholomew had recently settled.

He wondered why this had happened to him. It was clear that he was in no condition to go back to sea anytime soon. Having made his living as a sailor ever since he had left home, he wasn't prepared for any other trade. Besides, he only felt comfortable on the deck of a ship. Would he now be sentenced to life ashore?

Whenever he felt troubled, Columbus searched for an answer through prayer. But this time many months would pass before he would feel he had an answer and begin to understand his purpose.

Landlocked he might be, but memories of foreign ports and harbors were permanently stored in Columbus's mind. Employed now in his brother's chart shop, he turned the scribbled notes and rough sketches done by Portuguese seamen into detailed maps and charts. Christopher found that the journeys he created on paper helped soothe his longing to be at sea.

He was surprised at how satisfied he felt, stuck in another darkened workroom that was as stifling as the old weaver's shop was. But Bartholomew's shop was always full of people discussing their new ideas. Drawing tables were laden with quill pens, ink wells, T-squares, and paints, the materials that cartographers used to document the new horizons of an expanding  world. The walls were covered with outlines of countries and oceans that had been etched on fresh parchment sheets. Seamen and scholars stopped by throughout the day to retrieve their maps and charts, and they talked enthusiastically about their latest explorations down the African coastline.

Lisbon had become the navigational capital of the world, and there couldn't be a better place for a mapmaker—especially one as curious as Columbus. He was watching the world expand bit by bit at the tip of his pen, and he grew excited each time he added a new island, current, or landmark to his drawings.

But eventually he felt cut off from the sea, as well as from the people around him. Speaking only Italian, he had neither the language skills nor the social connections to mix with the Portuguese navigators. He wanted to talk in depth to these men who went to places where he yearned to travel. To do that meant he would have to learn their language. And so he did, setting himself the ambitious goal of becoming expert at three new languages as soon as possible! He chose Portuguese, so that he could talk to sailors; Latin, so that he could read works of the philosophers and scientists; and Spanish, so that he could speak to people of the upper classes, where the power and the money were.

Taking to books as he had once taken to ships, Columbus discovered not places, but ideas. His dreary mental fog gradually lifted as new visions of the world's geography came to him. He was fascinated to learn that the second-century astronomer Ptolemy believed that a giant continent stretched halfway around the northern hemisphere. Another scientist, the fifteenth-century cosmographer Pierre d'Alley, insisted that the Ocean Sea was not nearly so great that it covered three quarters of the globe, as most others believed. But out of all his readings, Marco Polo's book *Description of the World* captivated him the most. Polo's account of his overland journey east to the exotic land of China started Columbus thinking that perhaps a navigator could sail west and arrive in China too. There was no question among the leading scholars that the world was round. Certainly, Columbus concluded, the sea had to wash up on a shore somewhere.

Then one day he came across a line written by the great Greek philosopher Aristotle. It said: "Between the end of Spain and the beginning of India is a small sea navigable in a few days."

Suddenly it seemed that his idea might not be so outlandish after all.

1478

Staying on in Lisbon allowed him to settle down…not just with his books but also with a woman. Twenty-seven-year-old Columbus fell in love with Dona Felipa Perestrello, and she agreed to be his wife. She was beautiful, intelligent, and best of all, she shared her husband's love for the sea. As the daughter of a Portuguese admiral, Felipa understood and admired mariner men. She not only planned to share her life with Christopher, but also the papers and sea charts left behind by her father.

The young couple settled on the island of Madeira, a perfect location for a man who was looking west. Madeira was the most westerly of all known islands in the Ocean Sea, and its people were haunted by superstitions about the surrounding waters. There were tales of dragons and monsters and evil spirits lurking below the surface. Few dared sail far from the sight of land.

But Columbus relished the mystery. He and Felipa spent hours poring over her father's notes and maps to see where his journeys had taken him and what he had written about the places. More and more, Columbus was driven to prove that the Ocean Sea was no more dangerous than any other.

In time it became clear that he was setting a direction for the rest of his life.

Columbus became an avid beachcomber, stalking the sands of Porto Santo. He scavenged clues brought in on the ocean's tides that might shed some light on his new theory that the Indies could be reached by sailing west. He found bamboo reeds that looked like the kind that Greek philosophers said grew in India. Tree trunks washed ashore that did not grow anywhere in Europe. An intriguing piece of evidence was a crudely carved statue, unlike anything Columbus had seen before. Fishermen told him that two corpses with broad faces and narrow eyes had washed up on a nearby shore. These people certainly did not look as if they were from Africa or Europe. Columbus concluded that they must be Indian.

The clues, however, were not as important to Columbus as the *direction* from which they had come. Each find appeared after a storm and was washed up on only the westerly beaches of Madeira. He took notes on them, which he discussed with Felipa. Together the couple thought of one possibility after another to explain their origins.

Obsessed with this pursuit, Columbus spent hours mapping out streams and currents that he thought might be responsible, hoping to prove that the debris originated in the Indies.

For years he told no one of his hunches. He would have to gather more material in order to produce a convincing argument.

1481

There was much to learn in Madeira, but not enough to keep a restless wanderer in one place forever. The year was 1481 and Columbus hadn't taken an extended voyage for a long time. The king's service often needed skilled navigators like Columbus, who could take charge of exploratory voyages. He was soon called to the service, commanding ships down the African coast—and he accepted eagerly. He could almost taste the salt on his face and hear the sea hiss under the sides of the vessel.

Moreover, he welcomed the chance to impress the king with his piloting skills and to probe the waters he would one day sail across, trying to find answers to his ever-increasing list of questions.

Each night during these voyages, he would retire to his quarters and record what he had seen and felt. His notebook bulged with entries from previous trips. In his own words:

Iceland, 1477
I sailed in the month of February, a hundred leagues beyond the island of Tile, whose northern part is in latitude 73°N and not 63° as some would have it. Nor does it lie on the [meridian] as where Ptolemy says the west begins, but much further west.

Ireland, 1477
Men of Cathay, which is toward the Orient, have come hither. We have seen many remarkable things, especially in Galway, a man and a woman of extraordinary appearance in two boats adrift. It is said that the northern ocean is neither frozen nor unnavigable.

Now in the southern hemisphere, he would note the following:

Gold Coast, Africa, 1481
Perpendicularly under the Equator is the castle . . . of the most serene
King of Portugal, which we have seen. It [the region below the equa-
tor] *is not uninhabitable as others have said, for the Portuguese sail*
through this Torrid Zone and it is very populous.

He loved challenging the findings of past explorers so that he could move ahead with his novel ideas about the new shape of the world. Knowing that the Torrid Zone was habitable now gave him great license to pursue his dream.

Still, his ideas were those of a solitary thinker; no other navigator, nor Portuguese scientist, nor the king himself was thinking in the way that Columbus was. He knew that King John of Portugal had invested time and money into finding a trade route to the Indies by going east around the tip of Africa. Columbus's challenge would be to persuade the king to look in another direction.

Then one day a letter arrived that would change everything. Years earlier, Columbus had written Paolo Toscanelli, a noted Italian geographer, though he had long since given up hope of receiving an answer. But to Columbus's delight, Toscanelli wrote that he agreed that it was possible to sail west and reach the Indies. He said that such a voyage would be about 5,000 nautical miles. Toscanelli included a map, which showed how this distance could be easily broken up by stopping at the many small islands along the route.

Columbus was ecstatic. He knew that Toscanelli was known and respected by the court as a forward-thinking man of the day. To have him respect and agree with Columbus's theories would surely impress the king. There was little more Columbus could say or do now to prove it was possible to sail west and reach the Indies without actually going ahead and making the journey.

He would arrange for an audience with King John as soon as possible.

1482

Columbus strode confidently into the royal court.

"Your Highness," he began immediately, "I've come to offer you the shortest route to the Indies."

King John leaned forward. He looked interested but baffled. Stretching a huge map out for the king to see, Columbus marked a route that went west from Portugal across the Ocean Sea. None of the king's other navigators had ever suggested such a voyage.

"It is an intriguing idea," the king said, "but why aren't you frightened like the others? My men report strange winds and currents west of the Canaries."

"You must understand, Your Majesty," answered Columbus, "that I have pondered this idea for several years now and studied the writings of others. You must know that this is not a new concept. I have researched and now wish to actually prove my beliefs."

The king leaned further forward, curious now as to who else had entertained the idea of such a radical journey.

"Men like Aristotle and Ptolemy believed that the edge of Spain and the coast of India are close," he explained. "They estimated that the globe is covered with more land than water. I want to sail west," he said, pointing out the window where the sun was just about to set, "and find out how far the Indies actually are."

The king was interested enough to confer with his advisors. But after a few weeks King John turned him down. "There is simply not enough hard evidence," he said, "to make such a voyage worth my while."

Columbus felt him to be a fool. How could the king be so short-sighted? he wondered. He was, after all, ruler of the navigational capital of the world.

The king's decision made Columbus want to prove his theory all the more. He would go elsewhere for help...and go there immediately!

1483

Months of hardship followed. Felipa died quite suddenly, leaving Columbus a widower and the sole caretaker of their little boy, Diego.

There is nothing for me here, Columbus thought during his days of mourning. Filled with sorrow and frustration, he set off with his son for Spain. Starting over in a strange country wouldn't be easy. He had learned that when he began his life in Portugal. Only God walked beside him now, and it was in Him that he would put his trust.

Everything was lost now, except his strong will. If the Spanish king and queen, Isabella and Ferdinand, turned him down, he'd go to France. And if the French king said no, he'd go to England. He would not be deterred. He owed that not only to Felipa, but to himself.

A few weeks later, father and son crossed the border into Spain, weary and worn. What was he to do now? Where should he begin? To whom should he turn? As Columbus asked himself these questions, he spotted on a hill, a whitewashed monastery whose walls glistened in the hot Spanish sunshine. Perhaps he should turn to men of God for help, Columbus thought, as he clutched young Diego's hand and headed briskly up the dusty path.

The friars of La Rabida welcomed the man with the small boy and listened carefully to his story.

Several of the friars were wise and noted astronomers, pursuing their own theories about the size of the globe. To entertain such an intelligent guest was a joy for them, and it proved to be a lucky coincidence for Columbus. Not only was one of the friars, Brother Perez, confessor to the queen, but another visitor that day was Count Medina Celi, a member of the royal court.

"I have a mission that I must carry out," Columbus told the count, "to open a trade route to the Indies, and in the process, spread the word of God to heathens."

"Well if it's money you've come for," the count declared, "I think we can be of service to you. The queen always welcomes worthy proposals. I suspect she'll find yours fascinating. Perhaps tomorrow, we could head south together and attempt to set up a meeting."

Late that night, when he retired to bed, Columbus felt excited but dumbfounded. Was his good fortune merely happenstance, or could it truly be the work of God?

He slept fitfully, anxious for the morning.

1486

iego stayed at La Rabida while his father went off with the count, who helped prepare Columbus for his audience with the queen.

"She is about the same age as you are," the count said, "and of simple tastes. You will see that she is direct, serious, and goes about her tasks in a businesslike manner. As a devout Christian, she tends to listen carefully to those who demonstrate similar convictions."

An audience was arranged and Columbus soon found himself before the throne.

"Your Majesty," Columbus said, kneeling first to kiss the queen's hand and then rising so that they were eye to eye. "I've come to enlist your aid in spreading our faith to heathen lands."

"What is it exactly that you have in mind?" she inquired.

"I have cause to believe that if a navigator were to sail west across the Ocean Sea, he would in no time come upon the lands of Cathay and Japan."

"Where did you get your idea?" she asked. "No one has ever suggested such a voyage, and yet, the idea intrigues me."

"Your Majesty, the Portuguese seem obsessed with sailing the long way around...that is, going down around the tip of Africa. But I believe that by sailing dead west from Spain one would arrive at the same destination." He pulled from a pouch Toscanelli's sea chart and quoted from other sources that now seemed to back up his argument. "My intentions are noble, Your Majesty. If I should succeed, and I will, Spain will have opened a valuable trade route, I assure you."

"Tell me, Christopher Columbus, why are you so certain of succeeding in an endeavor that others would not even dare to attempt?"

Christopher, having secretly planned to make a dramatic gesture, pulled an egg from his pocket and placed it on a table. "Your Majesty," he said, "I implore you to make this egg stand on its end." The queen was astonished, but tried to oblige him by making a half-hearted attempt. When it was clear that she had given up, he lifted the egg from the table, cracked the bottom ever so slightly so that there was a flat spot, and set it down in the center of the table.

"You see," he said, "you can do anything you want if you know how."

"Your confidence and determination impress me," the queen said to Columbus. "However, as with every proposal that comes to me, I must discuss the matter with my counselors to see if they think a westward voyage is practical. And of course there is the matter of funds....I am not certain we can afford such a mission at this time."

Columbus remained silent, waiting for the queen to continue her statement.

"I will see to it that you have room and board and a salary until such time as we have an answer," she promised. "You will meet our scholars, mariners, and nobility to discuss your case, and perhaps further your knowledge."

And with that, Columbus was dismissed. He was encouraged by the queen's interest, and planned to enjoy his leisure time while he awaited her decision. The queen's court was filled with men well-versed in such sciences as geography, cartography, and mathematics. Columbus found his conversations with these men at once stimulating and restful.

1487-1491

ut he never intended for the rest to last as long as it did. One year stretched into two and then three. The waiting was interminable, a cruel treatment for someone with a passionate interest in discovering the secrets of the world. Always at the beck and call of the court, he was willing to meet with anyone to gain support for his voyage, even though most of the meetings ended in frustration. Time and again he appeared before the Talavera Commission, a group of the queen's scholars, allowing them to question him on his geographical knowledge. Having gotten used to doubters by this time, he listened patiently to their trivial questions: How could he be certain about the width of the Ocean Sea? Wasn't he fearful of sea monsters and boiling water? His calculations about the size of the globe made no sense. Every geographer knew that the ocean covered three quarters of the earth. Surely he would run out of supplies long before he reached the Indies, if indeed he arrived there at all!

It was almost impossible to answer questions based on superstition, myth, and out-of-date scientific calculations. Columbus, though disheartened, was not really surprised when the commission failed to produce a recommendation.

Finally, five long, frustrating years after Columbus had arrived at court, the Talavera Commission delivered its conclusions to the queen: "Columbus's promises . . . [are] impossible, vain, and therefore worthy of rejection."

Columbus wondered why they couldn't understand that many of their questions were unanswerable until someone actually set out to explore unknown territory. What about the queen? Why hadn't she had the good grace to reject his voyage in person? After all, it was she who had been so interested in the first place. Surely she couldn't have meant to so utterly deflate his spirit. Yet the more he thought about it, the more Columbus realized he should not have relied so heavily on her commitment.

He felt like a fool to have had such faith in the court. To spend one more day at the mercy of Spain would be too humiliating. He would leave behind the country that promised so much and had given him so little. It was off to France!

Discouragement weighed greatly on his shoulders as he trudged wearily overland, instead of sailing westward across the wide sea. But, as always, he walked on, steadfast in his faith. Once again he was led to La Rabida.

"What brings you here, Christopher Columbus?" a jovial Brother Perez asked as he watched his weary friend trudge up to the gate of La Rabida.

"It is over," Columbus replied heavily. "The Talavera Commission has found my voyage to the Indies unworthy. If I may just spend the night, I shall be off to France in the morning."

Brother Perez was shocked. "I cannot believe that after all this time the queen would give up her interest in such a noble mission. There must be another reason," Brother Perez said, hoping to console Columbus.

"Whatever the reason," Columbus said, shaking his head, "I cannot endure their insults and lack of respect for another moment. From the beginning I vowed to find someone to finance this voyage and I shall not give up now."

The very next day, after Columbus departed La Rabida, Brother Perez left for the royal court to request an audience with Isabella.

"Your Highness," he began, "forgive my interference in matters of state, but I have come to implore you to reconsider helping Christopher Columbus."

"Dear Brother," she answered, "everyone seems to think as you do, that is, everyone but my advisors. Only yesterday, my treasurer came to me with a similar request. He threatens to finance the journey himself if I do not see fit to decree it. What has so impressed the both of you?" she asked.

Brother Perez answered her with silence. Surely she must see that Columbus was different from the others. Here was a man with a God-given mission. She should applaud his bravery and courage by honoring his gifts and using his skills. In short, he should be permitted to fulfill his mission without further delay.

No one was more surprised than Columbus when a messenger from Queen Isabella intercepted him on the road to France and ordered him back to the court.

How dare they ask me back for more humiliation! Columbus thought angrily. After six and a half years he did not trust this new turn of events. And yet, he knew that a royal order must be obeyed. He had no choice but to return.

I will not glorify Spain for nothing, he thought as he trudged back again. If the Spaniards want my services, then they will have to pay dearly, with titles and honors and a share of the riches that I will surely discover!

It was an embittered Columbus who this time knelt before the king and queen, handing them his list of demands. Though shocked by its length, Isabella resolved to help him. She had made up her mind and there was no turning back now.

"I have notified the town of Palos to outfit three caravels and sup-
ply you with provisions and crew. You have my permission to begin
immediately with your plans to sail west. May God be with you!"
And so began the voyage that would change the world.

Columbus wrote in his journal on August 3, 1492:

Your Highnesses resolved to send me, Christopher Columbus, to the said regions of India, to see the said princes and peoples and lands and the manner in which may be undertaken their conversion to our Holy Faith, and ordained that I should not go by land (the usual way) to the Orient, but by the route of the Occident, by which no one to this day knows for sure that anyone has gone.

Your Highnesses commanded that with a sufficient fleet I should go to the said regions of India, and for this granted me many rewards, and ennobled me so that henceforth I might call myself by a noble title and be Admiral-in-Chief of the Ocean Sea and Viceroy and Perpetual Governor of all the islands and mainlands that I should discover and win.

And I departed from the city of Granada on the 12th day of the month of May of the same year 1492, on a Saturday, and came to the town of Palos, which is a seaport, where I fitted for sea, three ships well suited for such an undertaking, and I departed from the said harbor well furnished with much provision and many seamen, on the third day of the month of August of the said year, on a Friday, at half after an hour before sunrise, and took the route for the Canary Islands of Your Highnesses, which are in the said Ocean, that I might thence take my course and sail until I should reach the Indies, and give the letters of Your Highnesses to those princes and thus comply with what you have commanded.

Seventy days later, Christopher Columbus sighted land in the New World: an island he called San Salvador, in the Bahamas. At this very sighting, without knowing it, he ushered in the Age of Discovery.

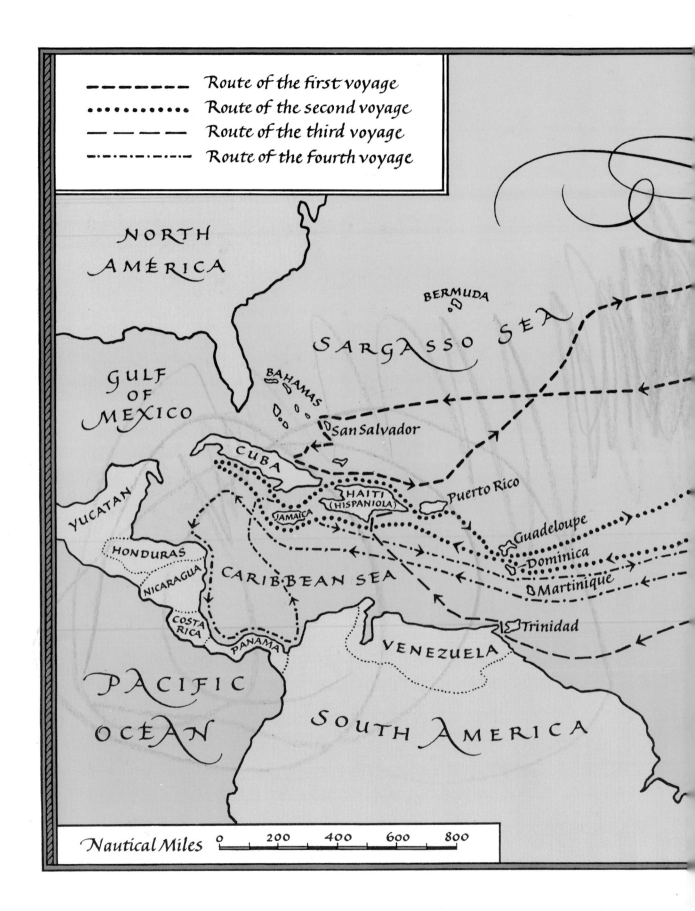

Route of the first voyage
Route of the second voyage
Route of the third voyage
Route of the fourth voyage

NORTH
AMERICA

BERMUDA

SARGASSO SEA

GULF
OF
MEXICO

BAHAMAS

San Salvador

CUBA

YUCATAN

HAITI
(HISPANIOLA)

Puerto Rico

JAMAICA

Guadeloupe

HONDURAS

Dominica

NICARAGUA

CARIBBEAN SEA

Martinique

COSTA
RICA

Trinidad

PANAMA

VENEZUELA

PACIFIC
OCEAN

SOUTH AMERICA

Nautical Miles   0   200   400   600   800

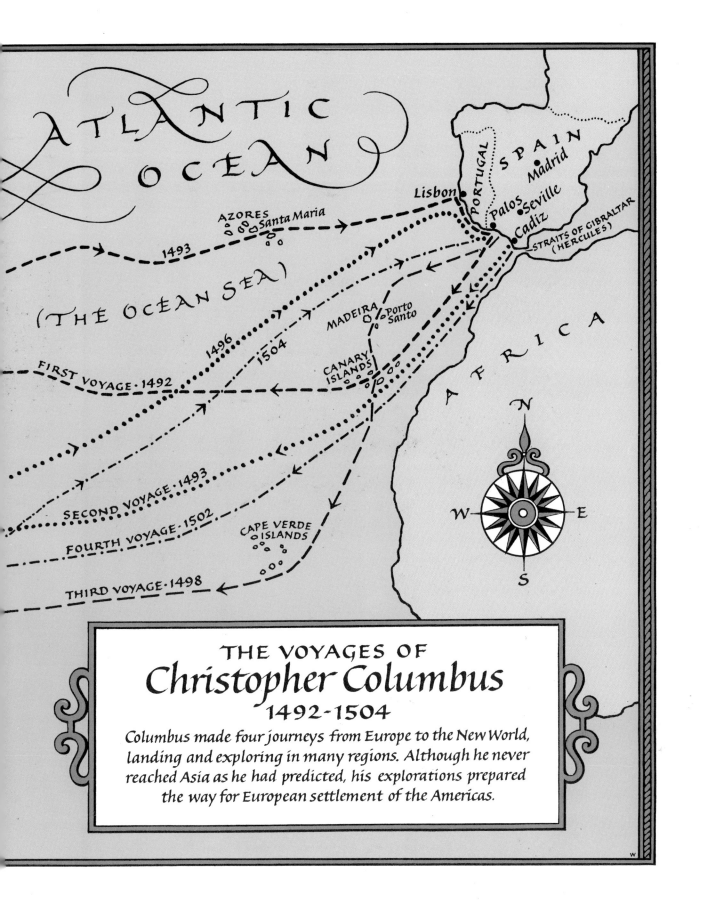

ATLANTIC OCEAN

SPAIN

PORTUGAL

Madrid

Lisbon

Palos
Seville
Cadiz

STRAITS OF GIBRALTAR
(HERCULES)

AZORES
Santa Maria

1493

(THE OCEAN SEA)

MADEIRA   Porto
Santo

1496   1504

CANARY
ISLANDS

FIRST VOYAGE · 1492

AFRICA

N

W   E

S

SECOND VOYAGE · 1493

FOURTH VOYAGE · 1502

CAPE VERDE
ISLANDS

THIRD VOYAGE · 1498

THE VOYAGES OF
Christopher Columbus
1492-1504

Columbus made four journeys from Europe to the New World,
landing and exploring in many regions. Although he never
reached Asia as he had predicted, his explorations prepared
the way for European settlement of the Americas.

Cast of Characters

Count Medina Celi · nobleman who first introduced Columbus to Queen Isabella

Bartholomew Columbus · brother who owned a chart shop in Lisbon

Christopher Columbus · (1451-1506) navigator, visionary, early explorer of the New World

Diego Columbus · son born to Felipa and Christopher

King Ferdinand · ruler of Spain and husband of Isabella

Queen Isabella · queen of Spain who finally granted Columbus ships and crew for his voyage of 1492

King John · king of Portugal who was the first to listen to Columbus's proposal and turn it down

Felipa Perestrello · wife of Columbus, daughter of a Portuguese admiral

Brother Perez · priest at La Rabida monastery who helped Columbus obtain a second audience with Queen Isabella

Paolo Toscanelli · Florentine cosmographer whose ideas about geography greatly aided Columbus's proposal

Places

Canary Islands · westerly islands in the Atlantic

Cathay · an old name for China

La Rabida · monastery in Palos where Columbus took refuge many times and whose inhabitants gained him introduction to Queen Isabella

Madeira · island in the Atlantic near Portugal

Ocean Sea · old name for the Atlantic Ocean

Palos · Spanish seaport where Columbus began his voyage in 1492

Straits of Hercules · the body of water between Portugal and Africa feeding out of the Mediterranean and into the Atlantic Ocean; now called the Straits of Gibraltar

Torrid Zone · the area around the equator